*The Pregnant Man*

# BOOKS BY ROBERT PHILLIPS

POETRY

*Inner Weather*     1966
*The Pregnant Man*     1978

FICTION

*The Land of Lost Content*     1970

CRITICISM

*The Confessional Poets*     1973
*Denton Welch*     1974

ANTHOLOGIES

*Aspects of Alice*     1971
*Moonstruck:* An Anthology of Lunar Poetry     1974

# THE
# PREGNANT
# MAN

*Poems by*
*Robert Phillips*

DOUBLEDAY & COMPANY, INC.
GARDEN CITY, NEW YORK
1978

The author gratefully acknowledges support in the writing of this book from the Creative Artists Public Service Program of New York State.

Thanks also to Michael Benedikt for suggestions which helped shape the book, and to Howard Moss and Erica Jong for suggestions which helped shape certain poems. Special thanks to Stewart Richardson and my editor, James Byers, for believing.

Some of these poems were first published in the following publications: AFFECTIONS HARDEN, Shenandoah, Copyright © 1977 by Shenandoah; THE EMPTY MAN, Paris Review, Copyright © 1974 by Paris Review; CHIMNEY-SWEEPER'S CRY, Poet Lore, Copyright © 1973 by Literary Publications Foundation, Inc.; THE MARRIED MAN, as THE MARRIAGE, and PENIS POEM, Choice, Copyright © 1972, 1977, by Choice Magazine, Inc., respectively; AFTERNOON IN PUBLIC LANDING and THE HAND, The Ontario Review, Copyright © 1977 by The Ontario Review; SWITCHMAN AT THE NORTH STATION, APOCALYPSE, AT THE SUMMIT, GIACOMETTI'S RACE, Modern Poetry Studies, Copyright © 1970, 1971, 1976, 1977 by Jerome Mazzaro, respectively; DECKS, THE STONE CRAB, BURCHFIELD'S WORLD, SOFT AND HARD, The Hudson Review, Copyright © 1978 by The Hudson Review, Inc.; THE STIGMATA OF THE UNICORN and BOOKS, Confrontation, Copyright © 1975, 1977 by Long Island University, respectively; SCISSORS GRINDER, The Centennial Review, Copyright © 1972 by The Centennial Review; PICASSO'S BOY LEADING A HORSE first appeared in Ball State University Forum, Copyright © 1966 by Ball State University; JONAH and FOOT NOTES, Attention, Please, Copyright © 1978 by Hearthstone Press; ARACHNE & MEDUSA, Helios, Copyright © 1977 by Edward V. George, Secretary-Treasurer, CASUS; THE INVISIBLE MAN, American PEN, Copyright © 1974 by P.E.N. American Center; KING MIDAS, North American Review, Copyright © 1975 by University of Northern Iowa; THE CULTIVATED MAN, American Review, Copyright © 1975 by Bantam Books, Inc.; DAPHNE & APOLLO, The New York Quarterly, Copyright © 1973 by The New York Quarterly Poetry Review Foundation, Inc.; A PREGNANT MAN, Encounter, Copyright © 1972 by Encounter, Ltd.;

FOR JUDY AND OUR SON GRAHAM

# CONTENTS

9

III     THE SACRED & THE SUBURBAN

*. . . And even in the man there is motherhood,*
*it seems to me, physical and spiritual;*
*his procreating is also a kind of giving*
*birth, and giving birth it is when he*
*creates out of inmost fullness.*

—RAINER MARIA RILKE


*. . . sitting at the table, thinking of the book*
*I have written, the child which I have carried*
*for years and years in the womb of the imagin-*
*ation as you carried in your womb the children*
*you love, and of how I had fed it day after day*
*out of my brain and memory . . .*

—JAMES JOYCE
to Nora

# I
# BODY ICONS

------------

*All thoughts and actions emanate
from the body. Every idea, intuitive
or intellectual, can be imaged and
translated in terms of the body, its
flesh, blood, sinews, veins, glands,
organs, cells, or senses.*

—DYLAN THOMAS
to Pamela Hansford Johnson

*Be not afraid of my body.*
—WALT WHITMAN

*And those members of the body, which
we think to be less honorable, upon
these we bestow more abundant honor;
and our uncomely parts have more
abundant comeliness.*

*For our comely parts have no need:
but God hath tempered the body together,
having given more abundant honor to
that part which lacked:*

*That there should be no schism in the body;
but that the members should have the
same care one for another.*

—PAUL THE APOSTLE

# THE SKIN GAME

Oh to be an onion!
Wonderful translucent
integuments, endless layers
of derma and epidermis,
membrane upon membrane
encircling the secret core!
Search for the heart of the onion
and find still another skin.
Search for the heart of the onion
and find yourself, crying.
The onion never cries.

> I am no onion. My skin
> so thin, stenographers
> type carbons of memoranda on it.
> Politicians draw treaties
> upon it. Barbarians shear it,
> wear it about hairy shanks.
> Enemies use it to make lampshades
> (and call that my shining hour).
> Hunters track me across the ice
> like Little Eva, and flay me,
> still alive . . .

Last week I bought a wet-suit.
I wear it all the time.
I clop down the street in it.
I flop down into bed in it.
Tough, rubbery, resilient,

it's like zipping myself inside
a deboned black man's hide.
It's being Huckleberry Finn
inside strong Nigger Jim.
It's not as many skins as the onion,
but it is one more.

# VITAL MESSAGE

The last thing I put on
    every morning is my

heart. I strap it to my
    wrist sheepishly, a man

with expensive friends
    exposing his Ingersoll.

But I strap it.
    Outside my sleeve it ticks

away the Mickey Mouse
    of my days. Some people

pretend not to notice. They look
    everywhere else but.

Some people touch it
    to see if it's warm.

It is. Warm as a hamster.
    One open-hearted friend

tried to give me
    a transplant. It wouldn't take.

I was left with my old,
    bleeding. A critic tried

to boil it in acid. It shrunk
    smaller than a chicken's.

One girl broke it. It crunched
    open, a Chinese cookie.

No fortune inside. One girl
    won it. She pats it,

a regular Raggedy Andy. And its
    worst enemy is me. I want

to eat it. Nail-chewers know
    how tempting! —a plump purple

plum just above the wrist.
    It bursts with a juicy sigh.

The skin shreds sweet. No seeds.
    So far I only nibble the edges.

There is more than half left.

# THE HEAD

Somewhere between your house
  and my house
I lost my head.

Not Walter Raleigh style,
  but gently—a child's
balloon suffused

with helium,
  adrift on the spring air
a surprised afternoon.

It floated over willows
  washing their hair
in silver pools,

sailed above clouds
  pale as cow's milk.
It drifted toward the city

over steeples and aerials
  prickly as a populous
pin cushion. It survived,

and came to rest
  outside your fourteenth-
floor window. It hung

around all day,
  a faithful dog
wanting in.

It peered through
        the dusty glass,
a prurient window-washer.

You were there.
        You never looked up
from your writing

desk. It wondered if
        you didn't care,
or if, miraculously,

you never once
        saw beyond the paper
sea to the blue beyond?

A head has no hands
        to knock with! So
it bunted,

a baby socking it
        to you in the womb.
No response.

At dusk it shrugged
        a neckless shrug,
mooned around the sill,

nuzzled the cool pane,
        a fish lipping
an aquarium tank.

Dank with dew,
        it shivered and dozed.
The sun rose, full of itself,

the head began
        to dwindle. Soon it hung
limp as a spent cock,

without the satisfaction.
        A banner in defeat, it sagged,
fell to the sidewalk

with a slight thud.
        No one picked it up.
Wrinkled, shapeless thing!

Unsightly as a bladder,
        unwanted as a used condom,
children kicked it around

like a dead cat. Dogs shat on it.
        Women dug stiletto heels
into it. Fourteen floors

above it all, you
        ran snow-veined hands
through fiery hair,

selected a virgin
        sheaf of paper, dipped pen
in ice, and wrote.

# PENIS POEM

I planted my penis
in the garden.
Like an Easter hyacinth.
Then watered it from a sprinkling
can. Then sat all night
on spiky grass, breathing
on it to grow.

        I prayed: The midnight sun
        will twitch it, sway it,
        lively, lovely, reaching tall
        and rubbery, Pinocchio's nose,
        Jack's beanstalk—

        Moonmaidens, come straddle it.
        Heavenly Cow, come milk it.
        Its seed will fertilize
        thousands of fields of light.
        Wherever I walk, it causes grain
        to grow. Oh, it will father
        generations of moonchildren.

        Torches, candles, fires
        are lit in honor of it.
        Its red head will blaze
        like a match. Dying women
        can rub it, be born again.
        I can rub it, be born again.

Like all my delusions
of grandeur, it never grew.

At dawn I carried it
into the house
between two fingers—
a slug from under a rock,
a macaroni from the kitchen floor—
myself rootless as a willow slip.

# HAND POEM

"My hand is my face."

—EDITH SITWELL

My hand shaved me
    before work each day

saved me in church
    high Holy Days

punched me in
    before work days

punched me out enemies
    after work days

earned me overtime
    hungry days

picked me guitar
    in town Saturdays

rowed me cross lakes
    crazy summerdays

pleasured me
    lonely winterdays

I was only a hired
    hand sometimes a helping

hand but always a happy
    hand till I gave

my hand in marriage:
    She grabbed it

kissed it powdered it
    wrapped it in pink

tissue paper, sealed
    it in Saks Fifth Avenue

cardboard, abandoned it
    to turn blue and die

deep in her vanity.

# FOOT NOTES

*For Robert K. Morris*

[1] "Oh, foot!" Great Aunt Nell cried
whenever exasperated.
Why *foot*? Why curse
that homely little pedestal,
pale as a toadstool?
The most humble of appendages,
it spends most of the day
hiding in someone's shoe.
No man in the subway
ever got his jollies
exposing his foot.


[2] The rays of the sun
are feet to help it cart
-wheel across Heaven.
The tips of the swastika
are feet: The better
to stomp you with,
my dear.


[3] O foot, O direct relation
-ship to earth,
O square root of under
-standing, you have grounded
me for life.

4 Billions of poems
about a broken heart,
not one about
a whole foot.

5 Pope's back, Cyrano's nose,
Vincent's ear, Marilyn's breasts—
Where is the person famous
for his foot? Only Achilles,
and Achilles is a heel.
For foot-prints, perhaps.
Thus Friday startled Crusoe.
Thus Longfellow lectured us.
Footprints show us where we've been,
cannot show us where we're going.
A foot has one foot
in the door of the future,
one foot in the grave.

6 Chinese used to bind them
to keep them small.
At night they worshipped
them under cool tabernacles
of bed linen.
At night they made love
to one another's foot.
Ahhhhh.

[7] We are all a race
of yearning feet.
Who will ever know
the loneliness of one foot
separated from the other?

# THE TENANT

First you carefully slit
my throat from ear to ear
and pulled the flap way back,
an entrance to the wigwam

of my chest, made semi-
circular incisions beneath
my arm pits, then carved clean
down each side. Foot braced

against my pelvis, you ripped
the whole flap down, skinning
this cat from chin to belly.
I was open, an unzipped sleeping bag.

You crawled inside, drew the flap to.
It sealed tight and final
as Hansel and Gretel's oven.
Now your games begin.

You tap tap tap on my tired brain
with a little lead hammer
like an aspirin commercial,
my bones clang and bang—

ice-cold plumbing attacked
by some irate tenant.
You voo-doo hat pins
into my doll-like heart,

kick against my belly: Feel
the world's largest foetus! See

the world's first pregnant man!
Every bite I eat nourishes you,

you funnel off every drink.
When I fast you suck my blood.
Already I've dropped forty pounds.
When I sleep you project old horror

movies in the theater of my skull.
When I wake you make my eyes mist,
spraying Windex on the mirrors
of my soul. I grind, blind Samson,

While you, a sailor, haul anchor,
pull my guts. You've an open-ended
lease, free heat and plenty of water,
the garbage is collected regular,

I'll never get rid of you.

# A PREGNANT MAN

Alone and at three
AM felt the first
twinge but thought
it something I ate
(cucumbers especially
big ones do that,
also radishes), but
at four AM the waters
broke, ran for a towel
to sponge the sheets
(what would my wife
say?) at five AM
the rhythms started
regular as Lawrence Welk.

At six o'clock called
my doctor but he didn't
believe me. Called my mother's
answering service but they
didn't. At six thirty
called a taxi but it
didn't, and at eight
on the button, open as
a bellows, clutching
the bedpost, screaming
between gold inlays,
a duck squeezing out
a Macy's Thanksgiving Day
parade balloon, gave birth
to an eight-pound blue

-eyed bouncing baby
poem. Spanked it to life,
lay back and had a drink.

P.S.

Two hours later
it died. You know
how it is with poems.
(My last one had two
heads and no heart.)

# THE EMPTY MAN

A cup before coffee, a shell
    after the scrambled egg,
I am a big nothing
    inside. A hole. A hideous
gaping vacuole. X-rayed, I
    reveal a TV set
after the repairman removes the tube.
    Nothing turns me on.

I tried to fill myself
    with Hope. It sprang
eternal, for a little while. But
    there is no future in it.
I tried to fill myself
    with History. But the past
is undeveloped, a thin black film.
    Nostalgia is not what it used to be.

I tried to cram myself
    with Literature. I became
a stuffed owl: Dickinson and Dickens,
    Diderot and Sappho, Colette
and Kant, Shakespeare and Etcetera.
    In the end,
they proved indigestible.
    In the end, they turned to shit.

I tried to fill myself with You.
    I funneled all your brunette hair,
brown-eyedness, energy, optimism
    and tits. All inside.

I poured you on. My ass
    had a hole in it. You leaked
away. Your beautiful essence drained
    like dirty bath water.

I tried to siphon off my Best Friend.
    His liver, his lights,
his action, his camera. I identified.
    I stole his talk, walk, wink,
stink. I sucked him through a straw.
    I, Dracula, succubus, lived
off him for months. The faster I absorbed,
    the slower I spun:
A running-down top,
    a drunken dervish whirl,
going everywhere, getting nowhere,
    my life staggered to a stop.
A decapitated chicken, it fell
    on its side. Help! I'm a key
-hole without a key. Help! I'm an eye
    without a hook. Can *you* satisfy?

# THE INVISIBLE MAN

No one looks up
when I come into a room.
Someone sits down on me
when I occupy a chair.
People stretch on top of me
when I lie in bed.
I am an invisible man.
My words, empty cartoon balloons.

My motives, totally transparent.
But there are advantages.
I don't worry about a wardrobe.
When people don't know you're there,
it doesn't matter which suit
you wear. Sometimes I like
being an invisible man.
I can eavesdrop on all,

observe all idiosyncrasies.
Last night I hunkered beside
your bed, smoked cigarettes
while you and your lover humped.
I blew smoke rings in his face.
He thought he was catching cold.
But mostly I hate invisibility.
It's being alone on a desert isle,

waving a raggy flag at airplanes
that pass and never land.
Of course, you could help:
You could acknowledge my presence,
come at me with your crayon set.

Look: scribble in my hair, my eyes,
my mouth, limb my body's tree.
Give some color to my life.
I'm a person!

(That too is a dream.)

# THE CULTIVATED MAN

I came from dust and must return,
but in between was living a dust-life too.
That seemed anything but fair,
dry roots stunted in a walking dustheap.

Even my sister, the moon, was not so barren,
her surface not so bald. My eyes? Instruments
recording thirty-five years' drought. My heart,
a forgotten avocado . . . Then you flew over

the field of my life like an emergency helicopter,
dropping your little Care Packages. I looked up,
saw you at the controls, brimming with more
carrots and nectarines than Carmen Miranda's hat.

I felt the twitch of the seed within the center
of the pod. I knew the industry of the beetle
pushing its dung ball. I tell you, the sun danced
over a mountain that day! The sun wore silver boots!

And that is when I vowed to farm
myself. To clear away the winter stubble.
There were truckloads of husk and tangle.
It was weeks before I saw my way clear.

Then I harnessed myself to my own plow
and broke the ground, each heave a beginning.
The neighbors came to watch and cleave together.
A cop had to come direct traffic.

Someone sold popcorn and soda-pop, even programs!
He's no farmer, the multitude agreed. I didn't care.

All that was beside the point. The point is,
I was a lout and had to cultivate myself.

I waited for the right time of month.
I waited for the moon to put on her best face.
When soil was ready and moon was ready
and I was ready, I fertilized with a fish.

I dressed that ground like a bride.
I sowed all my seeds. Some carrots, some nectarines,
but some notions of my own, too:
little red maples, because they are liveliest;

poppies because they make most seeds.
And now I sit and wait for rain and for you
to slip away from your yellow kitchen.
Come, we can dance in the furrows. We can hop

like two rain toads. Hop is a word like Hope,
only more immediate. I can milk the cow whose udder
is the moon. I can skin the hare that haunts
the moon. After this, I can do anything.

# THE MARRIED MAN

I was cut in two.
Two halves separated
cleanly between the eyes.
Half a nose and mouth on one
side, ditto on the other.
The split opened my chest
like a chrysalis, a part
neat in the hair.
Some guillotine slammed
through skull, neck, cage,
spine, pelvis, behind,
like a butcher splits a chicken breast.

    · I never knew which side my heart
    was on. Half of me sat happy
    in a chair, stared at the other
    lying sad on the floor. Half wanted
    to live in clover, half to breathe
    the city air. One longed to live
    Onassis-like, one aspired to poverty.
    The split was red and raw.

I waited for someone to unite me.
My mother couldn't do it. She claimed
the sissy side and dressed it like a doll.
My father couldn't do it. He glared
at both sides and didn't see a one.
My teachers couldn't do it. They stuck
a gold star on one forehead,
dunce-capped the other.

    So the two halves lived in a funny house,
    glared at one another through the seasons;

one crowed obscenities past midnight,
the other sat still, empty as a cup.
One's eye roadmapped red from tears,
the other, clear and water-bright.
Stupid halves of me! They couldn't even
decide between meat and fish on Fridays.
Then one began to die. It turned grey as old meat.

Until you entered the room
of my life. You took the hand of one
and the hand of the other
and clasped them in the hands of you.
The two of me and the one of you
joined hands and danced about the room,
and you said, "You've got to pull yourself
together!", and I did, and we are two-
stepping our lives together still,

And it is only when I study hard
the looking-glass I see that one
eye is slightly high, one corner
of my mouth twitches—a fish on a hook!—
whenever you abandon me.

# II
# IN CLOWN CLOTHES

---

*I acknowledge myself a clown . . .*
*But I've also discovered that the clown*
*and the angel are very close*
*to each other.*

—HENRY MILLER

# ARTISTS

## 1

PICASSO'S "BOY LEADING A HORSE"
*(after the Portuguese of Zila Mamede)*

It is a naked horse and a naked boy
who have nothing at all in their nakedness
except loneliness shared, and dim destiny.

No one knows whether the horse mourns the evening,
or if the boy's mourning somehow touches the horse.

When they draw near they are always withdrawn,
aloof from that evening to which they belong,
(in the grey plane that encloses them).

If from one or the other comes suddenly
clarion call or lamentation, we should know

it is because it is evening for both of them:
The boy's evening comes with the first shining star,
the horse's with the sight of hay—

Just two in time, more lonely with the dusk.

## 2

GIACOMETTI'S RACE
*for Herbert Lust*

Bone-stack
beanstalk
broomstick
clothespole
gangleshanks:
they are
the thin
man inside
every fat
one who clamors
to climb out.
Every jaw
a lantern.
Every face
a lean
hungry look.
Ancient
violence.
Violent
freshness.
Do not
trust them.
Do not
trust them.
But:
the beauty!

Tapers flicker
in vertical
air! Delicacy
of a hair!
Economy
of herring-gut.
Studies
of the minimal.
Learn
to love them.
Learn
to love them.
Water,
not milk.
Rail against
fear of paper
shadows. Teach
survival on
slender means.
Live
off the thin
of the land.

BURCHFIELD'S WORLD
*for John I. H. Baur*

In the late great paintings of Burchfield,
all nature goes round and around!
Cornstalks jig, crickets genuflect,
clouds flap like cawing of crows. Those
wild Burchfieldian nights! The wind
is a fleet of shrouds. Disaster
explodes from church-bells' claps, tele-

graph wires all shrill. Lie still. Lie still
and think about fear of the dark,
the mystery that lurks in the hearts
of trees, in the guts of all stumps
in still waters. Why is the air
so heavy with flowers tonight?
Why the cicada's nerve-music?

The night's alive with idiot eyes
of houses, a thousand wet houses
that rot. Look: frequent the alleys
the same as boulevards. God is
what you find under a rock, God
is the face of a hollyhock
in the late great paintings of Burchfield.

# FELLINIESQUE

"My wife, my mistress,
the Blessed Mother and I
dance against a cardboard sky,
join hands, gambol, sing,
shadow figures in a shadow ring.
I strut and fret, await the sun,
a middle-aged unholy Four in One."

# HUNCHBACK

"Pity
all the poor
bastards
who will never
know humility,
carrying
like a donkey
a burden
on one's back."

# IN MEMORIAM:
## THREE AMERICAN WRITERS

### 1

In a Victorian
gingerbread house
the color of vanilla
ice cream, pain
sat in a chair.
Pain drank amber
relief from a tumbler.
Pain's body was a rag
doll with the stuffing
gone. Pain took
my hand in her
one good one
(jerking jackhammer
style), said she
was working on a new
book. In her head
pain was.

### 2

He walked, talked
so swift we mortals
lost pace.
Thoughts came so fast
syllables tripped.
Greasy suit,
wrinkled hair, still

strode princely
across the Quad,
Francis to the birds
of academe.
Before he fell
he swore to kill:
Rockefeller
was shazzaming
beams from the Empire
State to scramble
his fabulous brain.

3

Encased in too too solid
flesh, she was an unserene
Buddha at the breakfast table.
Slander flew like knives.
Which was huger, herself,
her unhappiness? Yet after
olive and onion hour
she plucked a Greek record
from the air, set the raucous
rhythm go. Then three hundred
pounds did dance, did dance,
the lightest elfin fancy.
That body was a thistle
swaying on its stalk,
the face a little girl's.

1. *Carson McCullers*
2. *Delmore Schwartz*
3. *Shirley Jackson*

# TWO DRINKING SONGS

## 1

### ALCOHOLIC ON THE ROCKS

Overhead the dogs are flying.
Underfoot rocks are singing.
Behind me leaves are clapping.
Up ahead the house is dancing.

Oh, this lake is one helluva dry
martini. I dive for the olive.
At the bottom I find it
is the moon moon moon moon.

## 2

### DRUNKARD'S CREED

I drink,
therefore I am.

# SIX HAIKU

*For Graham V. Phillips*
*who first said the first one*

### 1.

"The cat spreads herself
    across my bed, like pea
-nut butter on bread."

### 2.

Tow-head dandelions,
    grey heads by end of August.
So soon we vanish!

### 3.

That silver balloon,
    the moon, drifts free of Him
whose breath gave it shape.

### 4.

That early riser,
    the sun, stands on a footstool
to observe the day.

### 5.

Pluck a daisy here—
    elsewhere in the universe
a great star trembles.

6.

To write too many
    haiku is to be nibbled
to death by small fish.

# AFTERNOON IN PUBLIC LANDING

*for Bill Heyen*

Being a man is harder
than being a woman, because

a man must deal with women.
A man is not the man he thinks

he is, only the man he is
in the eyes of a woman.

A boy bounces a rubber ball.
The afternoon grows cold.

The cat has caught a bird.
It flutters, will not escape.

My neighbor hangs ragged pant
-aloons upon the windowsill to dry.

I have accomplished nothing.
I have accomplished nothing.

# BOOKS

A book is so binding!
Hardback or soft, its cast type

type-casts, the shifty writer's
fancy set into iron-clad rule.

In them that Ophelia,
the imagination, ceases

to strew random flowers,
becomes statue;

the good-time girl shackled
within an iron maiden;

the spirited butterfly
pinioned under glass.

I have reread my books.
They were written by strangers.

# BEAUTY

*(after and including prose by Colette)*


        can no more be investigated
        than the butterfly wing.

        Abstain.

But: oh cold blue flame
(brighter than the peacock eye,
iris of the universe)

dwindling into the feathers
of the dewy wing,
how?

        When I put my finger on it,
        lightly, lightly,

        a trace of ash remains.

Lifeless. Weightless. Near-invisible.
The dishonored subject
flutters raggedly away.

# REVELATIONS

*for Bernice Woll*

1

APOCALYPSE

It will come as we have always known
it will come. But not as we have
always thought it will come:

Not with the sound of cornets,
the sibilant beat of feathered things.
No. Not so.

With the scream of sirens.
The soft meshing of gears on grease.

### THE VISITATION

A skeleton hovers at my door,
bony fingers beckoning.

He is not alone. Ghost-sheeted pygmies,
witches, crones taunt me, too.

The neighborhood children are hallowe'ened.
They trick and treat beneath that jack-o'-lantern,

the moon. So gay, these sacrificial children,
so happy, death-haunted, and doomed.

They are what they must become.
I fish candy from a bowl,

to sweeten the mortal voyage.
In the glass my cheekbones glow!

HAPPENINGS

Rounding the blank corner of my block
I stagger under sudden shock—
Red lights flash, arched hose streams,
fire-engine throbs, siren screams—
The head knows it is my house
long after eyes espouse
the truth. The neighbors'.
*Someone else.*

Disaster rarely clangs and wails
before one's door. It comes quietly, in the mail,
in the slight sigh of brakes that fail.
Swimmers disappear silently as the sun,
a mote captured in the X-ray beams
malignant. The telegram's dull collage
does not shout, it whispers
*You.*

### THE DARK SIDE

*(after and including prose by Robert Bly)*

| | |
|---|---|
| It comes dressed | in clown clothes |
| It has a tail | and lots of hair |
| It leaves no finger | -prints, odor of musk |
| It tickles like hair | in an African baboon's ear |
| It is the aborigine | in the fuel supply |
| It is energetic | as the young Mozart |
| It yanks open | unapproachable doors |
| It grows snakeplants | on ancestral graves |
| It is the beast | that will mate with anything |
| It drags death | to bed for dessert |
| It cries impulsive | old cave echoes |
| It is a four-hundred | -pound eating machine |
| It eats shadows | and white nightgowns |
| It wants to eat | the world whole |
| It wants to eat | me whole |
| It is inside | all of us, waiting |

# HARLEQUIN & COCK

*for Tom Baker*

### 1

Figure of night, bloodless Harlequin
identified by mask, fake motley,
is brilliant, but all but all buffoon.
At cock-crow he shrinks, hides, or like
some old Expressionist blinks at day—
cock of the night, no cock of the walk.

### 2

Cock, dawn-bird, sun-splendid in true
motley, decks the day out in feathers.
Like Matisse he stares unwinkingly
into the day's eye: of course he bears
Priapus' name, ready: unruined
as Cocteau, his song argues the first
glint, greets before the Resurrection
Christ, the world, his next recovery.

# III
# THE SACRED &
# THE SUBURBAN

———————————

*The sacred and the suburban often coincide.*

—RICHARD HOWARD

# DECKS

In the fair fields of suburban
counties there are many decks—
>redwood hacked from hearts
>of California giants, cantilevered
>over rolling waves of green
>land, firm decks which do not
>emulate ships which lean and list,
>those wide indentured boards which
>travel far, visit exotic ports of call.
>No. Modern widow's walks,

these stable decks, stacked with fold-up
chairs, charcoal bags, rotogrills,
>are encumbered as the *Titanic*'s.
>They echo Ahab pacing the *Pequod*,
>the boy who stood on the burning,
>Hart's jump into the heart of ice,
>Noah craning for a sign, a leaf . . .
>These decks are anchored to ports
>and sherries which mortgaged house
>-wives sip, scanning horizons,

ears cocked for that thrilling sound,
the big boats roaring home—
>Riviera, Continental, Thunderbird!
>Oh, one day let these sad ladies
>loose moorings, lift anchor, cast
>away from cinderblock foundations.

Let the houses sail down Saw Mill,
Merritt, Interstate. You will see
them by the hundreds, flying flags
with family crests, boats afloat

on hope. Wives tilt forward, figureheads.
Children, motley crew, swab the decks.
Let the fleet pass down Grand Concourse,
make waves on Bruckner Boulevard.
Wives acknowledge crowds, lift pets.
The armada enters Broadway, continues
down to Wall. Docked, the pilgrims
search for their captains of industry. When
they come, receive them well. They harbor
no hostilities. Some have great gifts.

# THE STONE CRAB:
## A LOVE POEM

*"Joe's serves approximately 1,000
pounds of crab claws each day."*

—FLORIDA GOLD COAST
LEISURE GUIDE

Delicacy of warm Florida waters,
his body is undesirable. One giant claw
is his claim to fame, and we claim it,

more than once. Meat sweeter than lobster,
less dear than his life, when grown that claw
is lifted, broken off at the joint.

Mutilated, the crustacean is thrown back
into the waters, back upon his own resources.
One of nature's rarities, he replaces

an entire appendage as you or I
grow a nail. (No one asks how
he survives that crabby sea with just one

claw; two-fisted menaces real as night
-mares, ten-tentacled nights cold
as fright.) In time he grows another—

meaty, magnificent as the first. And,
one astonished day, *Snap!* It too
is twigged off, the cripple dropped

back into treachery. Unlike a twig,

it sprouts again. How many losses
can he endure? . . . Well,

his shell is hard, the sea is wide.
Something vital broken off, he doesn't
nurse the wound; develops something new.

# SOFT AND HARD

The night they came to carry you away
it was your sacroiliac, not your mind.
Poleaxed on your bed of pain, unmovable,
you who never took aspirin cried out
then for novocaine, codeine, anything.
Two men had to lift you onto the stretcher
in only panties and bra. Black. Blessedly opaque.

Every light in the room glared, the outside
world inside at last. I saw how it looked
to strangers: dolls, magazines, stuffed bears,
real kittens underfoot, books books everywhere:
like the Collier brothers whose Bronx home,
after they died, was stacked with every newspaper
they ever read. The ambulance took you,

I was left surrounded by the wreckage.
Once, younger, we ran through the park,
saw squirrels burying nuts under fallen leaves.
"I think they do that to soften, not save them,"
you said. "To make the hard shells edible."
Dear one, how hard we tried to soften all
our edges with things. And by going underground.

# DAFFODILS

After too short
　　days in the house
their petals begin

to furl: banners, beached
　　starfish inching
their jaunty legs,

ancient suns
　　sputtering out,
aborted swastikas,

old billy goats
　　wagging gruff
goatees, Chinese gold

-fish trailing trans-
　　lucent fins, feeble
butterflies lifting

broken wings, owl-
　　brown moths, dead
on the attic floor.

## SUNDAY RITUAL

That silver gravy
boat was all
afloat with giblets
till Father helped
himself. His ladle
fished full fathom
five. Four children
bated breaths, waited,
faces clean and
wide as China
plates. We memorized
Father dipping all—
all the gizzard,
all the liver
parts—then saw
the lonely heart
get drowned in
his potato dam
before he passed
the burgled gravy
on.

# NURSERY RHYME

I rattle the bars
of my old play pen,
poop-poop in my Brooks
Brothers pants again,
puke mulled Pablum
on carpeted floors,
destroy all my toys
and clamor for more;
suckle the tit
when I tipple,
dentures locked
on the purpling nipple,
cry when I'm hungry,
cry when I'm cold,
cry when I'm sleepy—
I'm forty years old
till they visit!

Nana, Mama,
Auntie dear:
They castrate
with pinking shears.

# TRANSFER OF TITLE

It's mine now. I mash
the accelerator and the Buick
monsters up my expensive hill,

its 1959 dorsal fins
thoroughly outrageous now.
It's a fish out of water.

But new, this Buick looked razzy
as some henna-haired hussy, the mistress
you never had. Dirt-farmer,

dirt-poor, you cashed all your insurance
for it. Mother and Father
thought you'd gone mad.

Grandfather, your last fling
transports me through a world
I'm making, a world you never knew:

a neighborhood where color TVs
flicker sickly through every picture
-window, where Thunderbirds

come to roost in every drive.
It's quite the oldest thing
in sight, steel and chromium

symbol of my own relative
poverty. But I need it.
Its padded dash is a bosom

to comfort me if I fall.
Its directional signals
wink confidence for me.

This Buick's body is heavy as love.
Who would ever have thought
it would outdrag you?

You, who hoed one hundred rows,
then crow-barred the tin roof
off the garage all in one day?

It still burns hardly any oil,
while you lie hospitalized, anesthetized,
your points and plugs shot to hell.

# CORN FLAKES

That's all he knows
of food, or wants. Ten-year-old,
skin white as the milk
he pours into his bowl,
he and the flakes are flat,
a formica counter top,
scarcely dimensional.

Upstairs his mother is flat
on her back again. She passed
out sometime before his face
and teeth were scrubbed last night.
He filled the tub with tepid
tears. A hollow plastic
duck bobbed dumbly up and down.

That duck is broken in the head.
It lets the water in and drowns.
He watches it lurch, then sink.
Though it has lost its quack,
the boy won't let it go.
Together they've weathered
too many liquid nights of fear.

Whenever she doesn't tuck him in,
or scold him out of bed for school,
he rises and finds her on the floor.
Poor mommy. The box is easy to reach
and pour. They crackle. The shower
builds, sawdust in a bowl.
Last week I tried. I treated him

to steak, which he pushed aside.
"Corn flakes, please," he said.

# JIMMY'S CHICKY-RUN

They're racing again tonight!
Hotrods cyclone dust and clods
across the television screen.
I search the face behind the wheel:
Cool-assed James Dean rides again.

Saw it first at a matinee.
Itchy seventeen, my forehead
blotched rough as cinderblock.
Bought a nylon zip-jacket,
mooded around in James Dean red.

I was a rebel with a cause.
I have that jacket still.
Carefully closeted, it smells
good, like sweat and gasoline should.
The flick's been on the tube before:

Watch it every time . . . Tonight
it's changed, somehow. Jimmy Dean's
the kid who comes Fridays to cut
my grass. I fold my glasses,
finish my beer, and blunder off to bed.

# JONAH

*for John Logan*

Sailing the depths in my deep abode,
I rose to new heights of bliss:

having cast off what passes for this world,
why would I want to return?

I was always retiring; here, I was retired.
I resented daylight. But, my presence

made the whale sick. She spat me
onto dry land. You cannot imagine

the depths of my despair on leaving
that fishy belly. Day and night

I sulked the shore, hoping for her return.
Today I resigned myself to the walls

of this, your city. No holy ghost,
I ascend to no father anywhere. I feel

the sadness of Lazarus;
the curse of the reborn.

# ARACHNE & MEDUSA

### 1

Pity the poor spider:
life hanging by a thread,
long fingers forever weaving,
weaving, tenuous statements
that hang in midair, snap,
fall, get spun again.
No poet more frustrated
than she: she creates beauty,
yet must eat flies.

### 2

Whenever he approaches the marriage
bed, and she looks at him
—just so— the old metamorphosis
begins: a faint stirring,
a snake sleepily uplifting
its jeweled head in the sun,
a gradual turning to stone.
Thus for centuries women's glances
have turned men on. But only Medusa
hardened the whole man.

# DAPHNE & APOLLO

Because she was daughter of a river
and feared a cease of flow,
because she distrusted Apollo,
that baby-face fink, the way
some women distrust a diaphragm,
because her tits were lemons
and she longed for watermelons,
because she once saw her brother's
penis, thick as a turnip
and just as purple at the tip,

she prayed for help and just
as Apollo's knees were prying
her thighs, she turned into a tree.
A rather silly way to escape
love, wouldn't you say, even if
the tree were a laurel? Green
fingers trembled, her breath
was full of chlorophyl. The limbs
Apollo spread were leathery leaved.
The box he fondled a dry tree-hole.
What good was sweet-talk now?
He looked sad as a priest on Good Friday.
He broke off a limb for a souvenir.

By nightfall it withered worse
than a paraplegic's. But it *was* laurel,
so he bent it into a wreath.
And crowned himself King of the May,
conqueror of all he surveyed. You can do
that when you look like Apollo.
He didn't wear it in public, of course,

just camped it up before the glass
in his Bill Blass at-home costume.
At night it hung from the bed post
limp as an old jock-strap.
Weeks later, he was able to moralize
the whole affair, as Greeks do:

Happy is the man who can
clasp in one and the same
embrace the laurel and his love!
That was moral number one.
No achievement without struggle
and triumph! Moral number two.
As for Daphne, the lass with
the frigid air, she can't get enough:
She does it in the field,
day out and day in she's at
the old bump and grind— Up with the shoots,
down with the roots, here comes the sap,
busy as any sex maniac, pant pant.

# MIDAS: AN ENTERTAINMENT

Because he had an absolute gift
    for botching every occasion,

because he grew up in Bronx
    -Renaissance bric-a-brac,

because his mother always preached
    to marry rich and he didn't,

because his wife had a taste for gold
    -lamé and rhinestone harlequin glasses,

because the only taste he had
    was in his mouth:

Greedy-guts Midas cried out
    when Bacchus granted him one wish—

"Make everything I touch turn to gold!"
    You see how this would be problematic,

but Midas didn't. When the touch came,
    he became a boy at Christmas:

Toyed with a leaf, and it became
    goldleaf heavier than Cartier's best;

apples magicked into golden orbs,
    the house supports, pillars of gold.

The tackiest home in Forest Hills
    had fewer gewgaws than he, all in a golden

afternoon. What a talented fellow
    I am, Midas gloated

and ordered his sweaty staff
    to prepare a celebration feast

glitzier than Truman Capote's Plaza party.
    Midas' mother and wife gussied up

straight out of Cecil B. DeMille.
    Such a fantastic floral centerpiece

you wouldn't believe. It looked like
    Walt Disney had thrown up on it.

But the bread, when it came,
    would not break, and the meat would not,

and the cheese would not, even the red
    wine was gold: wine and victuals everywhere,

and not a bite to eat. Midas threw
    himself on the floor,

cried like a Miss America contest winner.
    Then raised his glittering fist to heaven,

begged Bacchus to relieve him
    of his golden load.

(There's a moral here, if you only look.)
    Bacchus sent him to the river

(at bottom he was fundamentally a Baptist),
    told him to rinse away his gilt.

He did, and that river runs yellow yet.
    Midas, in need of a hobby,

runs Lionel trains. On and on through the palace
    they race, while Mrs. Midas plays

out her martyrdom. She twists a lonely gold
    wedding band on one finger of one hand.

# THIRTY-EIGHT SUMMERS

Helen, her sun-dead skin
tanner umber the three months through,
knew desire as she knew
scorched sands of sundry beaches.

Even the coldness of the outdoor shower
pricking her conscience
could do nothing to cool those coals.
Drumming water against the tin
shower stall was sleet against
her heart's barricade.

Helen, when walking the edge of a fretting surf,
would feel the jab of love, sharp, distinct,
the throb of a bare foot that has run
too quickly over rough, nail-studded boards.

To look at the beach was pain enough:
couples everywhere laughing
beneath the saffron-streaked sky.
It made her dizzy, knotted in the throat.

Helen went crabbing one afternoon.
There was no one to help her bait
her safety pin with the dead fish head.
How she hated the dead fish head:
Its insolent eye razored into her body's marrow.

She recalled dry bleached wigs of seaweed
and raw, raw ribs of whale.
She dropped the frail line
into dark water depths below.

For thirty-eight summers she had known
the moist cool smells of wet cement;
nail-gouged sand and grit from her scalp.
Helen knew everything but the feel and smell
of love, and how to bait a safety pin hook.

# ON A SHELL

All the world is a Shell
service station. Now children
are sent out to the lube
bay to play. The grease pit
is the park, the pump isle
the ceremonial altar.
No more lindens or willows,
only pneumatic lifts
to hiss and limb the landscape.
Underfoot air hoses twine
thick as sweet potato vine.

Today, taking my constitutional
down James—James Street,
where Henry, Alice and William played
their fearful psyches and supped
from golden bowls—I passed
that baronial pile, the Everson,
pilasters filigreed as wedding cake,
and saw the hateful yellow sign
nailed to a tree like bleeding
Jesus: On this Site to be Built
Another Giant Super Shell.

# SCISSORS GRINDER

He
set spring
into motion each year
with his
wheel

No
storms came
down or screens went
up before his
fire-

works
children ran
to see sparks dance (in-
candescent angels
on pins)

For
nickels and dimes
his rotary righted every
hoe axe mower
marriage

Till
stainless
steel made in Japan
orphaned the ancient
cutlery

Then
no scissors etc.

just children came to love
the wheel with empty
hands

He
went. Never
came back this spring or last.
The seasons cleave to one
another,

don't
change, and
all the just-new knives
are dull. They blunt
the days:

life,
that old
case of knives,
has lost its
edge.

## "AFFECTIONS HARDEN"

*(after a misprint in a poem*
*by Richard Howard)*

". . . Affectations" you must have meant,
        or rather, they were what Auden meant,
in the context out of which you quoted him.

But affections harden too, Richard:
        run a strict course more damaging
than mere affectation, which whether

of speech, or gesture, is a false assumption,
        the unnatural assumed—
behavioral aspiration which consumes.

Affection, by definition, is a feeling
        or emotion defined, a natural
impulse swaying the mind.

The former exhibits the unreal,
        the latter settles a good will
or zeal. Both lay hold. Hardening

can be strengthening: *viz*. vulcanization.
        Not so with me. I lose in love,
gain the leathery slap of the glove.

Once I had a teacher, who encouraged
        cleverness, till she thought I became
too . . . too what? It's hard to say.

Once I had a friend, huge-hearted,
        mirthful, a clown. Fame calcified
his features; they took a hard line.

And once I had a lover, who stood still,
    a yellow willow in the snow.
Like Daphne, she closed all limbs to me.

What happens to the heart, hard hit?
    Affection, pressed, turns affectation:
indurate, enduring, a shell against the rain.

# THE EUROPEAN SCENE

*for Evelyn Shrifte*

## 1
### AT THE SUMMIT

A myriad carven statues
known only to the encircling air!

      At uncalculable points
      the profile of some little saint

gazes with bald marble eyes
onto vast indolent Lombardy,

      a pair of folded hands prays
      before bright, immediate Heaven,

sandalled feet planted
at the edge of the impossible abyss . . .

This whited world, lonely
as the snowfields of the higher Alps,

      sends with keen incision saintly limbs
      and spires to leap, to shoot,

assault the unsheltered blue,
their glow more glorious

      than that pitiless star,
      the Sun. Daily that orb staggers,

withdraws, dies—a wounded old general
within his tent of night.


But these sweet marble monks,
this youthful angelic population,

　　　unmelted, unintermittent,
　　　shines forever.

　　　　　　　　*Milan Cathedral, 1972,*
　　　　　　　　*after Henry James*

## THE STIGMATA OF THE UNICORN

### Tapestry I

Two noblemen, two huntsmen,
    a bray of hounds, and a young prince
trouble the bluebells of Flanders.
    They stalk the miraculous. The tracker signals.
Just ahead the virtuous beast
    dips his purled horn into a stream.
The waters instantly purify.

### Tapestry II

Goat's head, beard and feet,
    lion's tail and pride, the single
knurled horn—from his eye
    an unnatural blue light.
They ring him with their spears.
    He resists till he sees the decoy
virgin. Into their hands he commits
    his life. He falls upon his knees,
lays down his head upon her lap.
    They close in. They crucify.
Oh, the cry of the wounded unicorn!
    It shatters the bluebells.
It glitters in the air!

### Tapestry III

Mortal wounds cannot slay.
    The cock crows. The unicorn rises
again, in glory, in a field fabulous with flowers.
    Stigmata glow on a field of snow.
His face spells forgiveness, hope, immortality.

*Musée de Cluny, 1975,*
*fifteenth-century tapestries*

## 3

### CHIMNEY-SWEEPER'S CRY

Black my suit, black my tophat,
hands, face, black all black.
They stare as I pedal past
in a gang of sticks and brooms.
They tread the common stone.
I climb aloft cheerfully, descend
to sunless Hell: soot, char, old batdung.


Ah, only the crookleg stork sings
more sweet than I! I am
in my element; there's a school
-book proves man is most carbon.
It's in all that twitches!
Earth Mother's hands are pitch.
Fairer flowers spangle blackest soil.


'Twas the raven Noah first let go—
the raven, not the dove. Bah,
your white hero astride a white steed;
where are horse and hero now?
Lilies for a dead man's chest.
Black is lively, as here as now;
white, a faceless clock. Listen:


There is a northerly creature,
I know, the Abominable Snowman;
white raging in a whirl of white;
no blackguard's heart so vile as he.

I choose my broom, I lower myself.
Carbon alone becomes immortal diamond.
Alone through hell Christ comes to shine.

*Düsseldorf, 1972*

# A NOTE ON THE AUTHOR

ROBERT PHILLIPS was born in the State of Delaware, in 1938, and attended small Delaware schools. He holds undergraduate and graduate degrees from Syracuse University, where he taught. More recently he has taught writing at The New School and at the Putnam County Arts Center, and spent several years in West Germany. In 1976 he won a CAPS Grant in Poetry, and in 1978 a Yaddo Fellowship.

He writes reviews for a number of periodicals, including *Commonweal*, *The New York Times Book Review*, *Saturday Review*, and *Modern Poetry Studies*. For a number of years he served as book review editor of *Modern Poetry Studies*. Currently he is an Associate Editor of *The Paris Review*.

His essays on poetry are collected as *The Confessional Poets* (1973) and he edited *Moonstruck: An Anthology of Lunar Poetry* (1974). Fiction writer as well as poet, his highly praised short story collection, *The Land of Lost Content* (1970), prompted Horace Gregory to hail him as "the best of America's younger generation of satirists."

Robert Phillips lives in Katonah, New York, where for ten years he has been director of the poetry reading series at the Katonah Village Library.